THE POWERFULS 2 SAVE THE WORLD

THE POWERFULS – SAVE THE WORLD

Copyrighted Material

ISBN 978-1-3999-0969-3

………………. ………………

Author: Sebrina Spencer & Keisha Spencer

Illustrator: Shane Lewis

About the book

The book is about Cleo and her superhero family, who work together to save the world.

Cleo wins a prize of a lifetime, only to discover that she and her friends were in for more than just fun on their trip to NASA.

Cleo is not your average girl; she has superpowers and with the support of her loving family they will save the world.

THE POWERFULS – SAVE THE WORLD

THE POWERFULS – SAVE THE WORLD

Hi my name is Cleopatra Powerful, although my friends and family call me Cleo. This is my story of how my family and I saved the world. It was a bright sunny afternoon in Essex. I could not believe it; I had won first place again at the science fair. What made it even more special was that my best friends Elise and Ocean had come in second and third place. The grand prize was a trip for me and two of my best friends to visit NASA In Washington DC.

My mum was waiting at the school gates with a big box in her hands. There was a big red bow placed on the lid. I looked at her and said “is it a present for me”, she replied “yes”, handing the box to me. When I opened the box, inside was a beautiful Beige and white Chihuahua puppy.

"Thank you, thank you, thank you" I screamed, I had always wanted to have a pet dog. The look on my face said it all; my mum could see she had made me very happy. I said goodbye to Elise and Ocean and got into the car and we drove home.

THE POWERFULS – SAVE THE WORLD

The boys were play fighting in the kitchen and I just could not wait to show them our new pet dog. The whole room came to a halt as I introduce our new pet to the family. Dad came into the room

"who is that in your hands" he asked.

It is our new pet, what should we call him?

Martin shouted out "patch.

Marcus shook his head, "How about the name 'Prince'.

Dad said "Prince is a perfect name as we are from African Royalty.

THE POWERFULS – SAVE THE WORLD

My mum then looked at my dad and said "I like that name too; you can all call me QUEEN from now on", we all started laughing. I am so sorry I forgot to tell you my family have super powers. Last year when my brothers Malcolm and Marcus turned eight years old, they received their super powers.

THE POWERFULS – SAVE THE WORLD

THE POWERFULS – SAVE THE WORLD

You see my Mum; Harriet Powerful is one of the most famous female athletes in the world. She is a superfast runner and she can teleport, My Dad Nelson Powerful, played football for one of the top Football and Soccer clubs in the English Premier League, he is extraordinarily strong and can travel back in time. Malcolm can see into the future and Marcus can read people's minds. My super power is healing someone with one touch.

THE POWERFULS – SAVE THE WORLD

THE POWERFULS – SAVE THE WORLD

My mum and dad have always told us that our powers are given to us from our ancestors who were African kings and queens.

THE POWERFULS – SAVE THE WORLD

I explain to everyone that I was going to Washington DC next week, as I had won first place in the school science fair. I know what you are thinking, I got superpowers that is why I won. Well, you are wrong I really do Study hard; I love reading and learning is fun. People think it's easy being smart, however I do put the extra hours in revising, making notecards so that I can be the best. My dad looked at me and smiled and said "this calls for a celebration".

powerfuls

powerfuls

THE POWERFULS – SAVE THE WORLD

Dad decided to take us all to Hyde Park for a picnic with our new pet dog Prince. We loved driving into the city, there are so much beautiful buildings. My favourite will always be Buckingham Palace. Malcolm loves the London Eye and as for Martin he could watch Big Ben (The big clock) all day.

My mum and dad love driving into London, as we lived all the way in Essex. The city reminds them of when they first met training for the Olympic games.

THE POWERFULS – SAVE THE WORLD

The picnic was absolutely beautiful, I enjoy family time with my mum, dad and the twins, it is without fail the best and now with a new pet, our family was complete.

THE POWERFULS – SAVE THE WORLD

THE POWERFULS – SAVE THE WORLD

The day to go to Washington D.C had finally arrived, one week had went by, so quickly. After winning the science fair, it was all I thought about. I have been so excited I could hardly sleep, and neither could Malcolm, he had been dreaming of a big fiery rock coming towards him, for months now. I told him not to worry about it as Prince will protect him whilst I am away.

THE POWERFULS – SAVE THE WORLD

It was time to go, I took my suitcase from the car; Elise and Ocean were waiting for me in the departure lounge. I joined them and we waved to our families goodbye and off we went to the boarding area to get on our plane.

I felt so grown up getting on a plane without my parents.

Welcome To
NASA

THE POWERFULS – SAVE THE WORLD

When we arrived at NASA everyone was so nice to us. They really treated us like we were royalty. They had Oreo cookies with M&M's in the milkshakes waiting for us on our arrival.

"Yummy" Ocean said "I could get used to this", we looked at each other and all started laughing. We were given a tour of the spacecraft we would be travelling in.

THE POWERFULS – SAVE THE WORLD

After the tour they took us to put on our astronaut suits, they showed us how to operate them. We all looked so amazing in our suits, this was literally a dream come true.

1
2
3
NASA
NASA
NASA

THE POWERFULS – SAVE THE WORLD

Next they took us to the spacecraft as it was getting ready to be launched.

Ten, nine, eight, seven, six, five, four, three, two, one...

We have lift off.

Was I really going into space with my two best friends, this was fabulous and out of this world, literally.

THE POWERFULS – SAVE THE WORLD

The spacecraft was taking us on a tour of the planets in our solar system, we passed Mars, it was really red, then Jupiter, which had many stripes. Next we saw Saturn, with its rings of dust. Followed by Uranus which looked like a blue pearl and finally Neptune the planet is enormous and truly sea blue.

THE POWERFULS – SAVE THE WORLD

"Look at all these beautiful planets" I whispered to Ocean. "Wait, what is that" Elise shouted, pointing at something in the distance. Everyone looked to where she was pointing. Ocean's face looked scared, it was a big massive rock on fire and it looked like it was going straight towards Earth. It's a meteorite, explained the female scientist.

NASA

THE POWERFULS – SAVE THE WORLD

Everyone on the spacecraft was in shock, the male scientist tried to radio NASA control room, they did not respond.

"We have to turn back immediately and warn the others" shouted the male scientist to the other adults.

I overheard the grown-ups discussing that the meteorite was big enough to destroy the Earth. I knew my dad was extra strong and my mother was super-fast so I needed to tell them to see if we could save the Earth.

NASA

The female scientist told us to take our seats for re-entry back to earth. As soon as we landed, I used Coco's phone to call my mum. "MOTHER there is a meteorite coming straight to earth; What can we do to stop it? My mum told me to stay calm, and they will meet me near the NASA sign in five minutes.

THE POWERFULS – SAVE THE WORLD

THE POWERFULS – SAVE THE WORLD

I told Elise and Ocean to stay in the Control room, I could see and hear all the adults panicking. As I left the room, a tall lady shouted looking at a screen “it’s too late, it’s too late, how could we have miss this, why did none of the machines pick it up, this is the end of the world”.

NASA

THE POWERFULS – SAVE THE WORLD

When I reached the sign, my mum, dad and brothers were waiting for me. “How did you get here so fast” I asked, Malcolm laughed “mum teleported us”. They looked different; they were wearing different outfits. “They are fireproof,” said my dad.

“As soon as you got on the plane Cleo, Malcolm’s power told us about the meteorite hitting the Earth, so we had to get our new protective fireproof suits made” explained mum. The plan is to fly up and move it out of the direction of Earth.

THE POWERFULS – SAVE THE WORLD

THE POWERFULS – SAVE THE WORLD

Cleo put on her suit, “let's go save the world”, As soon as we got into space Martin and Malcolm could not believe how many stars there were. “Wow, space is so cool”, they both said at the same time. When Martin saw the meteorite he said it looked like a giant basketball on fire. Mum said “No, this is serious, let’s save the world”.

THE POWERFULS – SAVE THE WORLD

We all flew straight towards the meteorite; Malcolm and Martin floated to the left of the burning rock; it was massive. They tried to push it towards mum and dad, it moved slightly however, not enough to change its course. Let's do it together, mum and dad joined the boys. The meteorite was getting closer to earth. We had one last chance to move it.

THE POWERFULS – SAVE THE WORLD

THE POWERFULS – SAVE THE WORLD

I joined my family, “woof”, what was that sound “woof”, I heard it again, it was coming from Malcolm. “This was not the time for jokes, Malcolm” I told him, I went next him, his bag moved, then out jumped Prince. “What are you doing here”. He licked my face, ‘yuck’ I gestured. “Come on you two concentrate” shouted mum, who was helping Marcus push. I positioned myself next martin, dad came next to me. One, two, three, push, with my dad being so strong we literally pushed the meteorite straight out of sight. It missed the earth and continued into space; the planet was saved.

THE POWERFULS – SAVE THE WORLD

We all started celebrating by doing backflips, "we saved the world" shouted Marcus and Malcolm. Our first family mission was a great success, until our next adventure.

Love, peace and Unity!

THE POWERFULS – SAVE THE WORLD